D1516342

Blake

Passion Over Fear

Brittany Pitteard

1430 W. Susquehanna Ave
Philadelphia, PA 1 21
215-236-1760 | treehou ks.org

Cover model: Blake.Chanel

Instagram/Facebook/Snapchat- Blake Chanel

Website- blakechanel.wordpress.com

Prelude

The irritating alarm on my phone pulled me out of my sleep. I couldn't hit snooze because it was across the room. As I sat up, Twin wrapped his arms around me, "Call in today baby."

"I can't." I had already called in three times in the last two weeks, because of him.

"Whatever." He sighed, throwing the blanket back over his head. I walked over to my phone to disable the alarm. Peeking out the window I noticed my car was the only one in front of the house.

"Twin, is it cool if I take a shower? Your mom is gone."

"Is Demonte here?" He asked with the blanket still over his head.

"His car is gone."

"Aiight." I took that as a yes. I had taken plenty showers over Twins house so I knew where the towels and washcloths were. I hated using their bathroom though because the only way to close the door was to stick a towel between the opening of the door and the frame, while closing it.

I grabbed my work uniform, my make-up bag, went in the bathroom and began handling my hygiene. After drying off, I was standing on the rug with my back facing the door, stepping into my underwear as I heard the door open, I couldn't see a face but I heard Demonte mumble, "Gad damn dat's a fat ass."

I don't think I had ever been more embarrassed. I scooted behind the door and continued getting dressed. That way if the door was to open again I wouldn't be seen. If Twin wanted to see me from here on out he was gonna have to come to my house. Demonte knew someone was in the bathroom because the towel was in the door. I could hear him picking with Twin as I was applying my make-up.

"Yo girl thick as mud!" He said while laughing. I couldn't worry about it, it was either be ashamed or be late for work. I needed to leave by 9am and my phone was showing 7 minutes til. My makeup was acceptable by company standards, so I began unwrapping my hair. I could hear the front door close and heavy footsteps pouncing toward me. The door flew open to an angry Twin. The scowl on his face told me he was mad at me instead of his brother.

"You bending over for niggas now?" He turned his head sideways while asking.

"I had just got out of the shower, he had to see the towel in the door." I peeked down at my phone to see how much time I had, as Twin came into the bathroom. He lifted the top toilet and asked, "What the fuck are you doing taking a shower while that nigga here? I told you bout that shit."

"I told you he was here. I don't have time for this I gotta go. We can talk later."

"You got time for whatever the fuck I say! Fuck you think I am, bitch?"

My neck snapped around so fast, "Who you calling a bitch, fuck you." I grabbed my carryon bag off the floor when suddenly I couldn't see. Holding on to the sides of the toilet bowl, I used every muscle in my neck to try and break loose from his grip. I had been submerged in water and trying to keep my mouth closed but it kept flying open. Twin yanked my head up from the toilet hovering my face over the water. The water was burning my eyes. I took the deepest breaths I had ever taken in my life, because the way he was cursing I knew I would surely be going back under. I knew I would have to kiss my job goodbye, this would be the fourth day of me calling in because of him.

He let go of the back of my shirt and I slid down onto the floor, taking deep breaths.

"Clean this shit up and hop yo ass back in the bed and make it up to me." He said in a calm tone. I knew in that moment, it was time to go**, but it wouldn't be easy.**

Chapter 1

The Desires of My Heart

I didn't know where my feet where taking me, I didn't even know if this was what God wanted me to do. Night after night I prayed and kept getting the same answer. *Do what I need you to do and I will give you, the desires of your heart.* I pondered on that scripture because it was the only one that I could find, that didn't sit well with me. Mommy would tell us, "*pay attention to the scriptures that don't sit well with you and figure out why.*" Of course, she told me that when I was younger, when seeking God was the last thing on my mind. When I had nothing to lose and only myself to live for.

I had scribbled Psalms 37:4, "*Delight yourself in the Lord and he will give you the desires of your heart*" on a sticky note and stuck it to my dresser, bathroom mirror and my computer monitor. I didn't know what to make of it, but I knew what my heart desired, I just wasn't sure if it was in Gods will for me.

I had been employed with Sam, as one of her professional MUA and Skincare experts for five years. I loved my line of work but I felt I was using my talent, to make her successful. I was helping her sell her products and growing her business. Sure, before me, she had business, but mostly with women who were going through menopause. I was the one who came up with her promo deals and kept her relevant. She had no clue what was trending. I knew she needed me, but I also knew that I didn't need her. I knew that I could have my own business and I wanted to travel. I wanted Blake to be a household name.

I had invested in my own skincare line and had a consultant team to help my products land shelves all over the country.

My sister handled bookings, for *Blake Chanel* services. I knew it could be successful, that I was quite sure of, but whether the timing was right being another story.

It had been a week since I quit working for Sam and was moving forward with *Blake Chanel*. My sister, Bradley had come over to celebrate my new venture. She brought wine and made Alfredo. I tried to put on a happy face for her, but something was nagging away at my heart and I knew exactly what it was. I didn't have the strength to deal with my past.

"It's been a week and I haven't gotten one sale. I bet Sam hasn't told anyone about my business. What about my regulars?"

"Why are you even thinking about your regulars and why are you thinking about Sam? You told me that you wanted to become a traveling make-up artist. You can't do that if you're still thinking locally. You will become a household name before you know it and your regulars will find you. Facebook has a good platform for sharing information. You're the best, word will get around." She attempted to comfort me. Once hired on with Sam. Make-Up-Artists were forced to sign a contract that we wouldn't fish or take customers from her if we left or was let go. I knew they would be looking for me though. I wouldn't waste my time explaining that to Bradley.

Bradley, the natural brown haired, butter pecan colored twenty-one-year-old, was in her last year of college. Her main issues were homework and finding an outfit for the next game. Not that homework wasn't important but she had everything at her feet. Our parents promised us that whether we lived with them or not they would take care of us financially, until we were married or had a child. She didn't have to work; all she did was attend school and parties. I wasn't jealous, I was proud that she took advantage of her young life, unlike me. I just knew she wouldn't understand the value of getting the chance to make a teenager going through chemotherapy feel like a queen for just a moment.

"I guess it just scares me that this is my only source of income and I'm just sitting around waiting on someone to have a date or go to prom to get their make-up done. That is terrifying."

"Well, not only is Prom around the corner but you're act like you don't have money saved up. We have already prepared for a year worth of what if's. I hope you didn't think you would see immediate results. That's only gonna happen if you plan on sleeping your way to the top." She raised an eyebrow. "Embrace the struggle of your business so that you can appreciate your success. If it was that easy wouldn't everyone be doing it already? Come on B! Grind beats talent when talent isn't grinding. Of course, most people will only need your services when they have an important day coming up. That's where the grind comes in at. Make people need you. Get on YouTube and teach people about skincare and sell your *Blake's Correcting Mask.* Advertise your own flawless skin. Go down to the news station, do interviews. Your promo team is only going to do so much. You have to let people know why *Blake Chanel* needs to be a part of their skin care regimen."

"I know, I know." All of what she was telling me was the truth. I somehow knew that all the promotion in the world wouldn't give me the success that I yearned for, with *Blake Chanel,* without God blessing it. I also knew he wouldn't budge, until I obeyed him.

"So, what the hell is the problem? Like I'm sick of having this same conversation with you. It's a great idea and has been planned very well. I'm like almost over it already!" Bradley grew impatient.

"It's Zayden."

"What do you mean its Zay? I told you I don't have to go back to school until August. I'm your babysitter for free all summer long."

"What about when you go back to school? Then what? What if I get booked halfway across the freaking world in the middle of a school week?" I had nobody in my corner that could help me, besides Bradley. My mother stopped speaking to me when she found out I was pregnant out of wedlock and my dad shunned me because of her. My 30-year-old brother, Breon, is incapable of taking care of himself let alone a child. I don't want my son to be home schooled. I want him to experience everything about school, the good and the bad.

"Well I can sit out a year until you figure..."

"You can go ahead and swallow the rest of that sentence because that's not happening boo! You have one year left. I need you to finish that so that you can handle the financial part of the business."

The silence in the room began to create a tension. I stared at the oversized calendar hanging over my desk, as if I wasn't looking at it for the hundredth time. Nothing had changed, it was still blank. I had no upcoming events or interviews.

 The grey and black color scheme across my living room didn't help my mood. I could hear the central air humming about the walls. The room was so chilly that Bradley was using the sleeve of her sweatshirt to keep her hand warm against the cool glass. It was mid-May and we were sitting in the house in our winter clothes. The thing about living in Florida was that once you turned the AC off, it would take about 16 hours to cool the house down again.

"What about his father?" She said it. She said the word, that I had been dreading. What about Zayden's dad? I could feel the moisture forming under my breast, as well as my arms. Even the AC couldn't relieve me. This was the elephant in the room for us. I had never spoken about his dad to anyone, not even Bradley. I lifted the oversized bulb shaped wine glass up to my lips to hide the anxiety plastered on my face.

"Come on Blake! I'm your sister! We've got to get some things figured out, about Zay. Your business has been live for a week, we don't have time anymore. I know you want to do things on your own, but you need his dad now. Otherwise your business is going to suffer greatly. Besides, I don't want my nephew following you around watching you put makeup on people and shit. And he doesn't need you teaching him how to hold his nuts!"

"Pfffff!" I spat my red wine onto my grey rug. "How do you go from encouraging words and motivational conversations to nut holding, Bradley?" We both laughed. I took the rest of the wine to the head and prepared my emotions to relive these events as I mentally visited my past.

"I'll tell you, but I need another glass and you have to get this stain out of my rug because you made me laugh.

"Okay, I promise! I'll pour us more wine and I promise to take your rug to the cleaner's tomorrow!"

Chapter 2

Trouble in Paradise

I probably shouldn't have while I was drinking but I closed my eyes and said a quick prayer. I needed to prepare my soul to feel hurt and shame. I knew that this was the one thing that was stopping *Blake Chanel* from prospering. *Delight yourself in the Lord and he will give you the desires of your heart.*

The funny thing was, the moment I began to seek Jesus; the desires of my heart began to change. Before I cared to know who, he was, I couldn't see past the following week. I just knew I needed to get back and forth to work. I knew I wanted to be successful but I was shallow about what I thought success was. I wanted to live lavish and drive expensive wheels. I wanted my success to enable me to buy anything that I wanted. I had to go through some stuff, to realize what my desires would be.

I went ahead and told Bradley the truth about my son's father, but I gave her the PG version. She was still my baby sister; I didn't want to talk about my sex life with her. I remember every single detail about the day my son was conceived. I often wondered if I should have done or said more.

Past

I was 19 years old, still living with my parents. I had attempted one year of community college and dropped out once MAC certified me to become a professional MUA. I was there for a paycheck and I seemed to be making a nice amount of money without even being certified so I stuck with it and ended up developing a passion for it.

It was September, 2005. So far it had been a good day. I was off for the weekend and I planned to do nothing other than spring clean my room.

"Blake, you have company." My dad yelled from the front room. I knew it was my boyfriend, Twin. I went into the Livingroom to find him in a faux conversation with my dad. I say faux because I knew Twin was being fake as hell, however my father was enjoying their chat. That was dad being dad though, he pretty much liked everyone.

Pushing his glasses further up the bridge of his wrinkled nose, dad gave his feedback on TIP's new album, Urban Legend.

"No, no you got it all wrong Twin, he was way hungrier on the I'm Serious album than this one. This one's good, don't get me wrong, but I feel it's sounding a bit more, commercial than street."

"Of course, Mr. Jackson. If you don't go commercial who do you think is going to support it, the streets? Man, these guys out here that he was catering to would rather support their drug habits than spend money on an artist. They can get any bootleg guy to burn every song in the world. The radio will push something that's women and kid friendly and the squares will actually go out there and spend ten dollars on buying that album."

I leaned against the wall by the hall way entrance shaking my head. My dad stood tall and lanky wearing a red and blue flannel shirt with his favorite pair of dark blue wranglers. Every holiday I would buy him a pair of jeans but he would still find his way back to the wrinkled wranglers. The coolest thing about him was his high-top Nikes, even though they were bent out of shape. I never understood how he mastered the art of keeping the shoes as white as new but so badly bent. He had a head full of grey hairs that he kept cut short. Oddly, he was a hip-hop connoisseur. He purchased new albums every Tuesday. I would sit in the garage with him as he worked on cars and listen to music. He would rewind a verse and say, "You hear what he said, Bede?" Sometimes he would just pause it and ask what I thought the artist was trying to say.

I interrupted knowing that Twin would want me to. "Come on Twin." I grabbed his hand. My brother was laying on the couch watching TV. He and Twin never acknowledged one another. Dad went out to the porch to sit with mommy as Twin and I made our way to my room.

Twin and I had been dating since high school. He was tall and black as hell. He wasn't even an attractive dark, he was crispy looking. At first I couldn't stand him but he had come to my rescue so many times in and out of school, between guys trying to hit on me and girls just being mean. His personality along with the rescues, made him the best-looking man in the world. I soon got over his chipped tooth and dried out cornrows. Him coming to my rescue made my parents like him, even though he hated them.

Upon entrance of the room he pushed my head into the wall. After realizing what happened I grabbed the side of my head and stumbled over to my bed.

"Here you go with this shit Twin!" I could taste his hand slapping across my mouth, followed by an aftertaste of blood. Looking at my hand, I became afraid, but not so much of a beating. Sure, I didn't want to get beaten on but I was more so afraid for my family. My dad was too old to fight, he would for sure get hurt and I had never known for my brother to fight anyone but I didn't want him risking his life or his freedom over a guy that I had chosen to date.

"Shut the fuck up, bitch!" He whispered. My room was far enough from the front room, that no one would become alarmed. No one knew that this had been happening to me. In fact, we were "the favorite couple" out of all our family and friends. My family members didn't think much of my parent's relationship because they thought my mom made decisions for my father, never letting him think for himself. Even Bradley, despised their relationship. I was the only person, that I knew of, who saw something different. They were my favorite couple. When I looked at them, I saw a union between two black people, that wasn't held together by children. Even though my brother, sister and I were all grown, my parents were still having date night. They were still in love and very much connected. Unlike other people, finances did not define them. As children, we never got the "ask your dad" or even the "ask your mom". Most of the time they knew the answer was either yes, or no right off. If they didn't answer, they would say ask me later or we will talk about it. That to me was a real authentic union. I didn't see a lot of *complimenting, or asking how each other's day was. I didn't see much intimacy maybe a peck on the cheek here and there, but it wasn't normal for me to see. In the same breath, I must say I've never heard of or seen my father lift a finger to harm my mother let alone raise his voice. My mother gave him the same respect, they never put each other to shame and never spoke of a chore that the other may not have done. I watched my mother get the five beer cans that my father left sitting on the living room floor, from the night before, without mentioning that she had done so. I watched my father clean my mother's platinum hair shed, off their master bathroom counter top while rapping lyrics to Plies, "36 Ounces". She never complained about his loud rap music and I never heard it playing in front of her Pentecostal sisters. My cousin said she'd bet money that my parents argue all the time, when nobody is around. I thought, isn't that the point? Isn't it healthy to debate or be heard? Isn't it healthy to not do that in public? They all were missing the point. I guess I understood it at a young age, because I was being abused. I appreciated everything around me but nothing that was of me. I felt like everything that I created was fraud even if it was just advice. What my parents had, was companionship.*

As Twin yelled at me, I would think this can't be love. My parents had real love.

"The fuck I tell you about walking around these niggas in them spandex bullshits, huh? You aint gone be satisfied til yo punk ass brother stick his dick in you while you sleep one night." He spat.

"He is my brother, aint nobody off that bullshit!" I yelled.

"Bitch, shut the fuck up!" He got in my face. "So you talking back? Don't make me close this fucking door!" I didn't say anything. I knew if

he closed the door, what would happen. He would take me into my walk-in closet and beat the hell out of me with whatever he could find. Adapting to these situations, I stopped storing stilettoes in there, being hit by a Jordan shoe was easier to endure.

"That nigga in there has a dick and he's twenty-four fucking years old. He aint getting no pussy, he living off porn in ya momma basement. You walking round dis mufucka wicha flat stomach and onion shaped ass. Looking like a fucking cola bottle and shit. He prolly watching you walk around so he can't whack off. Nigga as far as I'm concerned ya daddy probably is too but I'm a give dat nigga a pass cause he so fucking corny. The next time I catch yo ass walking around in something tight or short, I'm beating yo ass in front of whoever. If yo punk ass family try to help you, I'll fucking kill em!"

I kept my eyes on the floor. I learned that if I looked at him while he was angry, he'd give me something to cry about. I could look at him with a blank face and he'd assume I didn't give a fuck. The easiest thing to do was to just stare at the floor, anything but him.

"Bitch give me yo phone, you aint getting this mufucka til you learn how to dress!" He demanded. I tossed him my razor phone from under my pillow and he left. I knew I wasn't in love with that fool, I was more so afraid of leaving.

I remember watching an episode of Maury when the women were being abused by their mates. Someone on the show asked one of the ladies, "How can you say you're afraid to leave him because he may hurt you, when he's hurting you anyway?" She also added, "If you think he will hurt you if you leave, I'm here to tell you that he will kill you if *you stay." The lady didn't respond and kept holding her head down under a man's command, who wasn't even on the stage. I was sure that the real her had already died long ago and she was only a breathing body. That was the way I was beginning to feel.*

I lay flat on my bed and took in what had just happened. I wondered what would happen if I told my parents about the beatings. More than likely, they would call the police. They wouldn't be able to arrest him without proof or my confession. He would consider me a snitch for wanting to stay fucking alive and he'd send me indirect messages that through mutual friends. People all over town would probably feel sorry for me and say what they would or wouldn't have done. My friends would call me stupid. For my own reasons, the beatings sounded better than going through all of that. At, least I knew what things set him off and could attempt to deflect them. My main issue was the fitted clothes. The problem was no matter what I wore, my ass was going to stick out. I used to go through this with my mom when I was in high school and now that I'm an adult and can wear whatever I want, my man wanted me in a Mumu.

****

"Knock-knock." mommy decided to say instead of knock. "Telephone Blake, it's Leah. She said your phone is off, where is it?"

"I left it at work." I lied.

"Oh well here ya go, just make it fast because Sister Lisa, is picking me up for bible study." She whispered.

"Hello!" I snapped. I was so irritated by Leah calling my mom's phone.

"What up B? Why you aint answer for me?" She was too excited for what I was feeling in that moment.

"Hey, I left my phone at work, what's up?"

"I wanted to know if you wanted to take yo stale ass out tonight?"

"You know what, yes, I will go! Me and Twin got into it and I need to get out of this house."

"Girl what yall got into it for? Yall lovebirds don't ever fight."

"Not up for discussion!" I shut that down. Leah was my girl and all but she lived for drama and that I could not give her. I needed an outlet just someone to vent to, but the way she told me about her cousin who married a guy ten years younger than her, and her aunt's secret drug problem, I knew my drama would be a sure thing for every ear that was in her path.

"Oh, well whatever it was I hope you leave his funny looking ass alone. Girl, he doesn't let you go anywhere and you be getting off the phone all fast and I still be having shit to tell you about."

"Okay Leah, so do you want me to go or not because if this is going to be the conversation the whole night, I would rather stay home.

"Okay, okay! I'll be there around ten." She exclaimed.

I went out to the front porch and handed momma her phone. She asked the dreaded question of the week, "Care to join us for bible study tonight?"

"No, thank you." I answered the same way every time. I wouldn't mind going to church, if we were going to dad's church. He was a member of a Full Gospel church and my mother was Pentecostal. It wasn't the church that bothered me it was the façade that she put up. We all had to stand a certain way, no earrings no makeup, no cutting hair and never pants. I had to go through too much of changing what made me who I was, just to get in the car with Sister Lisa.

I went through my closet and pulled out a few pieces of clothing that still had tags on them. Things that I thought I would be wearing, until Twin started whooping my ass. One was a red jumpsuit with the back cut out. I put it on and it fit like skin. I remember it having the perfect cuppage for my size c breast and it was the one body suit that didn't give me camel toe. I couldn't wait to wear it somewhere.

I needed a break from my normal. I needed to breathe and I was going to look damn good while doing it. I did a side take in the mirror and I know exactly what Bradley meant when she'd say, "a nigga could sit a glass of water on that ass, Blake!" I was blessed with beauty, but I was so much more than that. The bedroom wall that surrounded my window was smothered from ceiling to floor in trophies and metals that I had earned from running track. I had certificates for perfect attendance and honor roll.

I wasn't sure what my future held if Twin was in my life holding me back. I couldn't even say thank you to the cashier at the gas station without him flying off the handle.

Spinning around for the back view of my outfit, making sure that the fabric wasn't cut too low, I noticed a thick purple bruise going up the middle of my back.

"Blake!" My little sister gasped upon entering my room.

"Bradley, get out!" I yelled.

"No, what the fuck? Yo, I'm telling D..."

I gripped her up by her shoulders, as hard as I could and covered her mouth. Her eyes began to water. Using my skills from running track, I lounged toward my bedroom door, pushing it closed with my big toe. I pulled her in my closet and shook her, in attempt to get her attention. Bradley was frantic and upset and she had every reason to be, but we didn't need to alarm anyone. Pulling her in the closet was a go to move for me, growing up with siblings. Anytime they were crying because of something I had done to them and I wanted to hush them before it got to our parents, closet we go. She was used to it. Oddly, it was Twin's go to area for me as well.

I slowly let go of her and she covered her mouth up with her hands. Once I was sure she was going to stay quiet, I removed my full *body length mirror, the calendar and my two sun hats from the wall and showed her the random holes that Twin and I created. She just stood there and stared at them like she was in an art museum. I stared at them as well, as all five holes replayed themselves in my head, reminding me that I had once again escaped death. I hugged my little sister. I was past the point of tears but I didn't like what my sister was seeing. I knew that she had put me on a pedestal and thought that I would be stronger than this. To me, I was being strong because I was keeping the family safe.*

"Listen, Bradley the police will not do anything. He would have to get caught in the act and even then, they can't hold him forever." I whispered. "All he would do is get out and come after me and what kind of a life is that to live? I don't have time to be running around looking over my shoulder?"

"But, what kind of life is getting the hell beat out of you? You are playing the dumbest fucking game in the world, Russian Roulette!"

"I'll tell you what it is, its strength. It takes strength to endure that. To carry that secret because I don't want to put my loved ones in harm's way. Do you know how many times he has threatened to kill everybody in this house? It's better this way, for now." I knew she wasn't falling for it but she nodded to agree and left the room. I tried on a few other outfits and noticed that he had hit me in certain areas so that I wouldn't be able to wear anything that revealed certain body parts. I eventually settled for a white tank and a pair of ripped jeans. I put on my white strappy open toe stilettoes and called it a day. Wishing I hadn't cut my bangs, I rocked them with a loose top knot bun. Trying

to dress up my simple look, I threw on my gold door knocker earrings and some clear lip gloss. I was just happy to get some air.

Chapter 3

My Cake and Eat It Too

Leah was right on time and as always, overdressed. She had on a short black cocktail dress, that had about ten thin golden chains hanging from the neck of it, that dangled down to her waistline.

"Aw, you look cute Leah."

"Thanks chick, get in, we got a long drive."

"Who's party is it? I should have asked that first to make sure it wasn't any of Twin's acquaintances.

"Girl, momma woke me up out of her sleep this morning talking bout go to the gas station and get a roll of toilet paper. I was so pissed. But you know ya girl, she don't go nowhere if she aint decent!" she referred to herself. "I was glad I had just got my hair rolled, and I had on my cute lil Dereon sweat pants." She smacked her lips and waved her *fingers all around like it was helping her describe how cute she was. She was already draining the life out of my sore body.*

"Girl, whose party, is it?" I rushed.

"Dag, you rude?" She mentioned, followed by a slow eye roll, but it sounded like a question. I knew this was a bad idea. I couldn't wait to ditch her ignorant ass at the party. I wouldn't care if she left me, I would call Bradley to pick me up.

"So, as I was saying. I get to the gas station, the one by Twins house, with the old red paint?"

"Yes, I know!" I stressed. She had irritated me all over again by mentioning his name.

"Well, there was yellow tape all around the doors and shit. I aint know what was going on at the time. So, I was about to pull off just as this motherfuckin tight ass, black Bentley pulls up on the side of me and ask if I know anything about what happened?"

"I was like nope. I just woke up. Then, he was like his lil family got shot while he was at work this morning, but he was gonna survive. So, he steps out and gives me his card and said if I hear anything to call him. You know me, I was like, what if I don't hear anything? He said his girl would kill him but he had single friends and they were having a party tonight. He told me bring some friends but I aint taking Terri ugly ass nowhere, with her flip-flop-wearing ass. But anyway, girl, he winked at me twice when he said he had a girl."

"O...kay, so?"

"So, bitch a dude was in the passenger side, I took it as maybe his girl is that dudes sister or she knows him well so he winked to let me know he wanted me." I nodded to get her to shut the fuck up.

"Can we listen to some Jay Z?" I asked. She sucked her teeth and granted my wish.

Heading out of Leigh High Acres and into Miami, Leah turned into a suburban neighborhood. Upon entering the gated community, I noticed cars parked along the winding road in front of the bare desert. I was hoping that wherever we parked at was close to the house party because I had been hearing about panther sightings. I could run but I was no match for a panther.

As we got closer to the inner circle of the neighborhood it seemed like the homes became more grand, taller gates, longer driveways, higher roofs and a better stone.

A car pulled away from where it was parked on the side of the curb and Leah swiftly moved in. The long line of cars behind us let us know how they felt about it, using their horns. Leah hopped out and sassed them.

"What to do den, hoe? What to do bih?" She threw her hands up at the oncoming cars. This bitch was about to either get us killed or laughed at for acting ghetto as hell.

We were about one minute from the party. I could see people standing out and inside of the gated lawn. This had to be the main attraction on the block. It was at a dead end and took up most of the land. I became ashamed at my attire.

"Girl I wish I lived out this motherfucker. You know what, new goal! Fuck all these hard ass years of school to not get the job I want. I'm a marry me an ugly mothafucka with some money. Some quiet, boring ass dude that don't like going places. I'm a marry his ass, rock his world and drive to the hood on Fridays and get some dick from the thugs. Yasss!" She snapped her fingers a few times and sashayed up the drive up. I laughed so hard. I didn't think it was funny, I just knew she was serious.

"Yea its nice out here." I agreed. I was in deep thought. Her mentioning marriage made me think of Twin. I wondered what he would say if he knew I was out. I knew he wouldn't find out because after the beatings, I wouldn't see him for about a week.

"What you mean it's nice though? This is the shit! This is the Hood dream baby!" She stated, matter of factly. The difference was I didn't live in the hood per say. I grew up in a predominately white neighborhood. We didn't have the same backgrounds and we didn't have the same goals. We only shared the same high school. Dad thought it would be healthy for us to go to public school. Leah just made me laugh a lot. I loved how free spirited she was. She did whatever she wanted and said whatever she thought. She wasn't afraid of what people had to say about her and I respected that. She was the friend I would party and maybe shop with. She just wasn't my go to for deep conversation or advice. I wouldn't share my ideas with her because she couldn't see past today. Everything she did and every move she made was to make it through the present day. I was trying to set myself up for the future, screw today, today was already happening.

"I mean it's nice, it's the shit!" I gave her what she wanted. I got excited with her about materials. Living out there was just not the goal for me. I wanted to go to LA. I could imagine my life as a *Celebrity MUA*. Moving into a gated community, was too small of a goal for me. Dad would say be careful when setting goals not to set them too low, you might mess around and hit them.

Everybody looked like they were dressed for a red-carpet event. I saw tuxedos, ball gowns, diamonds, pearls and cufflinks.

"I'm not going in there!" I said to Leah, speaking through the side of my teeth while smiling. "I'm the only person with jeans on, not even the men are wearing jeans!" I started to sweat.

"Girl you can go sit in the car cause I'm going to find me a husband."

There I was left standing in front of a palace, looking like a fish out of water. I didn't want to sit in the car knowing that she'd stay in there all night. I could at least go inside and have a drink. I was hopeful that they wouldn't ID me because I was only nineteen. Deciding to take a chance, I went inside.

The front double doors to the house where already opened. People were passing in and out. I went inside and I couldn't tell a difference in the temperature. I guess I imagined it would be cooler but it felt the same as outside. I took the room in, trying to locate the bar. The ceilings were enormous. There was a door to my immediate right, that seemed off limits. People pushed past me smelling like money. I took a few steps forward to get out of the doorway and noticed a black railed spiral staircase that led to a balcony where more people were hanging out. The room was dim so I couldn't see the floors well enough to determine if they were marble or granite. The great room was empty of furniture, except for a long, white leather, s-shaped sectional. There was one couple smooshing around on it. I couldn't make out what they were doing but they had to be high off something the way they carried on. I saw about four women next to the bay window, make a b-line to the door with a glass in their hands and noticed they were coming from the corner of the room. There was a cluster of people in that corner so I figured I may as well step over. Maneuvering slowly, I weaved through the bunch, to a tall thin guy leaping over a wooden bar.

People were demanding and ordering and every time I thought the bartender was looking my way, I would attempt to open my mouth but it was like I was invisible. I didn't want to become so noticeable that I'd remind the drunk people that I was out of dress code and technically a minor. So, I laid back. I turned around to see if I saw Leah anywhere but I didn't. Surprisingly, about eighty percent of the people in the room were black. It was a mix of professionals and street guys. The women looked like models. The other twenty percent of people were Latina.

"Aye mami! Chu, need it?" The bartender asked me pointing to the drinks.

"Two shots of Tequila and a Key Lime Pie Martini, please. I opened my clutch to get my money out of the inside zipper, when papi Chula reached for my hand to stop me from paying. He winked at me and handed me my drinks. This night may not be so bad after all.

"For you, because the jeans mami!" He winked again and smiled. I blushed. He was handsome as hell, with all gold bottom teeth. I took my free drinks and went back toward the door. The wall by the staircase was empty, I figured I'd make that my spot for the night. I had made myself comfortable there and would be able to catch Taronda if she walked past.

Anthony Hamilton was pleading to Charlene through the speakers. I was about to have a panic attack because that was Twins song. I took both shots of tequila to the head and sat the shot glasses on the floor by my feet. Leaning against the wall I felt my body slowly transition to a different level. Everything in me began to relax I felt my eyelid gain weight. I was glad "Charlene" was fading away in the speakers as it was followed what sounded like a live orchestra chiming through the speakers and I knew it was "Look What I Got" by breakout artist, T.I.P.

Closing my eyes, I could imagine this piece being recorded. I envisioned an orchestra on one side of the room and a dope rock band on the other side. Both musicians from different worlds, but having one thing in common, their love for creating. My hips took it upon themselves to sway from left to right and then into a circular grind. My free arm flew up into the arm and began snapping with the beat and randomly pointing at nothing, but in rhythm with each lyric I spat. In my head, I had transformed into the female version of T.I.P and felt untouchable. I was finally having a great time and didn't want it to end.

I opened my eyes to this fine motherfucker standing directly in front of me. He wasn't dancing, but his head bobbed to the beat while he grinned and watched my lips recite the lyrics. He joined me in the recital as I kept grinding, knowing that he was completely entertained.

He got nose to nose with me as we both rapped in unison, "fuck ya lil thoughts and that lil house you think I'm in/ get a Benz I'll value yo opinion then." I giggled and he caught my bottom lip with his. Suddenly everything around, us was nonexistent. I was so drunk that Twin could have bumped into us and I still wouldn't stop kissing John Doe. Kissing like we were drinking water from a fountain, saying so much without speaking a single word. Using his hands, he scribbled everything he wanted to tell me along my voluptuous frame. My vulnerability accepted his request for my love. He stopped kissing me but stared into my eyes. I stared back with confirmation. Still matching my stare, he reached with one hand, down to one of the decorative holes in my jean leg and yanked at it, causing the rip to expand, revealing most of my thigh. I still gave him a straight face. I wasn't sure why he went for the rip but I was digging this rough motherfucker. He grabbed my hand. I dropped my plastic cup and followed him.

He led me outside and around the drive-up into a three-car garage. After unlocking the passenger side door to a black SUV, he instructed for me to sit there. He began sucking on my lips again. I was more intoxicated by him than the liquor. It was the unfamiliar feeling of being wanted, attentive and attractive. I took my shirt off while he assisted in removing my jeans down to my ankles and entered my world. Just standing within me, no grind pattern just the stillness of him caused a current. Facial hair, a wide nose and a chocolate tone had me loose. He stood on the outside of the truck as my leg dangled around him. Not receiving the rhythm, he wanted he stood me up with him, bending me over the seat. I held onto the seat for the support as we mimicked apes. He suddenly stopped, like he heard something but I was too drunk to care. I felt his hands tracing the bruise in the middle of my back, all the way up to the smaller bruises by my neck. Leaning in close to me he began kissing my reminders. The bruises were reminders that I belonged to Twin and that if he knew what I was doing in this very second, he would add to the collection. His tongue felt like silk dancing on my skin. I had never had sex with anyone other than Twin. I figured since it may never happen again, I should make the most out of it.

Once we finished I rushed into my clothes and went back toward the house to look for Leah. I found her standing at the front double doors. She claimed she had been looking all over for me. I told her she shouldn't have left. I held my clutch over the ripped part of my jean leg to avoid any questioning from her.

"Well there was no sign of who lives here and I'm bored as hell, all these guys are lame, so let's go."

"Okay, but first you have to let me get something to drink for that long ass ride home." Mystery man had sobered me up. I knew I would never see him again and he would only exist in my imagination.

In my reality, I was far more submissive to a man, than what was considered natural. Submissive to a guy who beat the crap out of me whenever he thought about it.

I had finished my Key Lime Pie Martini and could feel it pouncing through my body by the time we got to my house. I unlocked the door to find my brother sitting on the couch in the dark.

"Why you sitting here in the dark?" He replied but I was too drunk to hear him or ask him to repeat himself.

I removed my shirt as I stumbled into my room. I took the first seat I could get to which was the chair upon entrance, I fidgeted for the light switch. I bet it took about five minutes for me to remove one shoe. Once I had them removed I began walking over to my bed...

"Fuck wrong witcho jeans, bitch?" Twin had been sitting on at the foot of my bed.

"How did you get in here?"

"Where the fuck you been? You all drunk and shit! Who is the nigga?"

"I wasn't wit no nigga, I was with Leah!" I said in defense. I knew I was in for it but at least my body was numb. I could probably even fight back.

"Aw ok. You was wit Leah, hoe ass? So, Leah is the nigga? You fucking Leah, is what I'm hearing?

"Twin!"

"Nah, you say you wasn't with no nigga? Lay yo stupid ass across this bed then, and let me smell my shit and see if somebody been in it."

"Before I knew it, my brother came flying across the room knocking Twin onto the floor. I shrieked. I didn't want my family putting themselves in danger because of my inability to leave Twin.

Bradley came from her room dialing 911 on her phone.

"You have to come now! Somebody's going to get hurt." She pleaded.

Meanwhile, my brother was beating Twin relentlessly and I was totally surprised. Twin Lay helpless, on the ground covering his face.

"You can fight a woman but you can't fight a man, huh? Bitch ass nigga!" My brother looked possessed as he continued hitting Twin.

Daddy pulled me, Bradley, and momma by the arm, yelling for us to go to the porch. Momma started asking what happened but I was so surprised by all the events that had taken place that I couldn't even answer her. In that moment, it had dawned on me the reason why my brother was still awake and in the front room. Bradley had told him everything.

It was happening too fast. I was numb as I replayed Bradley seeing the bruises on my back, then fast forward to my brother knocking Twin onto the floor. The rest was blurry. I felt a drizzle of rain fall onto the porch stoop. Magenta then violet serrated the streets into the 2am quiet. The sirens were so loud that it brought me out of my trance. I didn't know if rain was on my face or if I had cried. I couldn't feel anything. I could see my mom mouthing put a shirt on. I didn't move. Bradley removed her house coat and put it around my shoulders.

What had I done? If I wouldn't have gone out, all of this could have been avoided, I thought to myself. My brother going to jail tonight would be a sure thing, and it was all my fault. They wouldn't take Twin, he hadn't even put his hands on me, he had only yelled at me. I could now hear my heart beating, over the sirens. I grabbed the sides of my head trying to stop the throbbing. The screen door opened one cop came out. The door closed. The door opened again and out staggered a bleeding Twin in hand cuffs, being ushered by another cop. My eyebrows probably touched my hair line as surprised as I was. I ran into the house. And fell into my brother's arms. Once the police ran Twins name it came back as the person of interest for the shooting at the gas station Leah went to earlier that day. The shooting of the clerk, that I would get cursed at for speaking to. The shooting that Twin did, allegedly.

"I'm so sorry!" I cried.

"What the fuck? You don't have shit to be sorry about! He's a sorry ass nigga! If you feel guilty in any way, you need to get some counseling lil sis." Those words echoed over and over time after time in my head. I knew I was messed up. I kept it a secret that, I felt like I was at fault. I never spoke Twins name again to anyone. I knew that I wouldn't be able to hide the way I felt. I didn't want my family thinking that I needed counselling. I was ecstatic that Breon didn't have to do anytime for beating Twin. The problem was they couldn't hold him forever.

Chapter 4

Tell Me I'm Dreaming

Snapping me out of my day dream, Bradley asked, "So basically, Zayden's dad is still alive? That's mainly all that I heard." She was so cute the way she tried to make me feel that she didn't judge me. I was blessed to have her.

"I guess. Well...I hope so!"

"Well we need start trying to find him cause honey you have a business to run."

"That is going to be impossible. I just told you I didn't have his name."

"Okay, tomorrow we are going to take Zayden to day camp and then were driving to Miami."

"Ok." No use in objecting, besides with her in my corner I knew that I could do anything.

I went outside to grab my *Blake Chanel* merch, when I realized that my mailbox was stuffed with mail. I was waiting on a few stores to reply about acquiring shelf space. If I could get Walmart, that would make my night. I stuffed them in my carryon that held my skincare line stash and raced to the bathroom locking the door behind me. I wasn't hiding the fact that I applied, from Bradley. I just rather be disappointed alone. I hate for someone to feel sorry for me.

I closed the toilet lid and took a seat. Taking a deep breath, I rummaged through about eight envelopes. I finally got down to a piece of paper that was folded in half. When I opened it, I could feel my heart chasing my gut. My eyes danced quickly from word to word trying to race to the end. It read.

I am here for my son or your life you make the choice.

Twin

Jumping off the toilet I threw the crumbled note in the toilet. I watched for the ink to escape the paper, but it didn't. In a panic, I flushed the toilet, but it wouldn't go down. Even if the note was flushed it wouldn't change the fact that Twin, still thought my son was his, and he knew where I lived. I didn't even know that Twin had been released. I Plunged the toilet until it went down and threw the remainder of mail on the back of the toilet and left the bathroom. I could feel myself hyperventilating. Telling Bradley what was going on would be a mistake. Keeping this to myself for now, I would watch our backs and hope to snag some out of town gigs. The route my business was taking in its first week, didn't give me hope that it was going to happen. I needed Zayden's father more than ever.

Chapter 5

The Search Begins

"This the house?" Bradley asked.

"Yep, this is it!" I got so nervous. For some reason, every time I get nervous about something, I become more aware of small things that I wouldn't normally. Bradley's car smelled like new leather and I remember her feet being bare as she pulled into the drive up. Sitting directly in front of us was the infamous three-car garage.

"We should go." I panicked.

"Blake get out."

"What if he's married and they have a family and a dog and what if I'm..."?

"Yeah, but Blake is not married, so Blake needs to worry about Blake and Zayden. My nephew deserves a father just as much as anybody else. So, are you going to get out and stand up for him or would you like to drive all the way back to Lehigh, while you regret being a punk ass?"

I sucked my teeth and rolled my eyes. Striding up to the door in a pair of jeans and a fitted Laker's t-shirt with gold flat sandals. I wore my hair up, the same as I did on the night of the party. Before we could even get to the large double doors, they were pulled open by someone from the inside.

A short dark skinned guy with a head full curly hair appeared, with a welcoming smile.

"Ahh. Rachel?" he stuck his hand out for me to shake.

Attempting to speak louder than the beating of my heart I replied, "Um, my name is Blake."

"Blake, hmmm. Are you here to interview for the maid position, I don't remember getting any emails with your name. I'm happy to interview you anyhow." He said, looking like Carlton from *The Fresh Prince of Belair.*

"Actually, I am here for a different reason." I cleared my throat and said, "I am looking for the father of my child."

He snickered as if he didn't want me to know he was tickled.

"Must be some mistake no, *father of my child*, as you put it, is here."

Bradley must have known a lump was forming in my throat because she chimed in. "I apologized Mr...."

"Kendrick."

"Mr. Kendrick, maybe you can help us. My sister, came to a party here and please excuse me, but she and this guy slept together. It is what it is. She never got his name and now she has a five-year-old son that belongs to him. Did you live here around that time?"

Kendrick's facial expression changed, perhaps the mention of a child made him care.

"Excuse my rudeness please, come in. Stepping inside and it was just as I remembered. In fact, nothing had changed. The white s-shaped sectional was still planted in the middle of the room. "Follow me."

We made the first right into an office.

"Have a seat."

The office was small. There were two classic brown leather chairs with gold prongs beaded around the edges of their back. The nerve of someone to stretch such hideous choice of carpet about the floor. He sat in a high back chair, making him seem taller than he was.

"So, Ms. Blake, just for a better understanding and in attempt to help you as much as I can, I need to recap. You came here, a few years ago. You forgot what this man's name is and you have no contact information? Did he speak about where he lived?"

"We, um, actually didn't even speak to each other."

"Huh? Wow, okay. Well, how do you expect me to find him out of a few hundred people?"

"Well, I think that even if he wasn't the person who hosted the party, he was very close to the person who did. Because while all the guest were parked alongside of the street, this guy was parked in the garage."

"Ha!" He exclaimed like found a clue. Why didn't you say so earlier? I've been renting the home out for about ten years now. So, you're lucky I keep in contact with all my clients. Do you remember the date?

"It was either the 21st or 24th of September 2004. I don't remember the day of the week."

After tapping a few keys on his desktop and a few swipes through his iPad, he scribbled an address on a sticky pad and slid it over to me.

"Go to this restaurant at 9am and ask for Ashlee Frank. Good luck on your journey."

Bradley, so focused on her phone, began walking extremely slow. I was standing by her car as she was still making her way down the walk way.

"Oh God, Oh God, Oh God! Blake someone prepaid for your services! They paid a holding fee for your bridal package, along with the *Blake Chanel Regimen* as bridesmaid's gifts.

"Are you serious?"

"Oh, my God Sissy! It's in Tennessee. She said she hopes you will consider her because her original MUA had a family emergency and it's only a three-week notice for fifteen girls. Please say yes. I haven't been anywhere since school has been out. Me and Zayden could have a room separate from you and you won't even know we're there. I promise I'll even rent a separate car, please?"

Little did she know; she didn't have to beg. I was ready to get on the first thing smoking to get away from Twin. I was over joyed. Just when everything in me wanted to give up and tell my old boss, Sam, that I had made a mistake, things were turning around.

Chapter 6

Fake Love

I was so lucky to have Bradley. She was my only friend and the only family member who still spoke to me. Everyone else was too intimidated by my mom to even ask about my well-being. The few friends that I did have loved the idea of me but they didn't care about me. I was always the friend that was floating. I wasn't doing horrible for myself, but I wasn't doing well either. If I continued to float they would continue to encourage the limitations that I put on myself. The moment I wanted more the more they would try to knock me back down to floating.

A painful memory would be that of my pregnancy. *I was at the lowest point in my life that I had ever been. I was twenty years old and due to my abusive relationship, had missed my teen years. All my friends had their own places and cars, I had neither. I was still working at MAC. I made decent money because I had no bills to pay. I guess I was single, because even if I wanted to, my family would forbid me to date Twin. The only thing that I was happy about was his incarceration. I would think about that and my world would light up, I would become a dreamer. The possibilities, opportunities and the blessings that Twin stood in front of, were at my feet. My joy would be disturbed with letters that Twin would send to Leah's house for me. He spoke of his innocence in the shooting and apologized for the way I, made him, hit me. I sincerely hated the air that he inhaled. After three months of me not responding, the letters turned into hate mail. He'd tell me how fat I was and that big butts weren't in style and nobody would want me.*

They couldn't lock him down forever. Nobody even had proof that it was him from my understanding. I was so weary of hearing anything about him that I stayed away from any conversations pertaining to him. I needed to come out of that depression. My plan was to focus on my career and move to LA and send for my family. It was my fault that I had put us all in danger and I was going to get us out.

I knew I was pregnant when I missed my period. Bradley sat with me as I took a few different brands of tests. All of them were positive and I wanted to die. Me getting away from this devil was easy, but taking his child away was not.

"What are you going to do?" she asked.

"Abort it!" I didn't think twice before answering.

"No, the hell you're not!"

"Seriously? I screamed. "The father is locked up and mommy said the moment we start having kids we're out of here! Where the hell am I gonna go? I can't go to Mac with my nose and face swelling up and my skin breaking out here and there! Nobody is gonna want their makeup done by me!" I panicked. I hadn't noticed mommy standing in the doorway.

The look of disappointment on her face alone made me want to swallow my words back down my throat. I wanted to look away from her, but I just couldn't.

"Get Out!" as she attempted to raise her voice, the softness in it cracked. You have twenty-four hours to pack all of your things and go."

Tears were pouring down to my breast, Bradley was yelling at mom, I was looking around at all my things. Where would I take them. How could I afford an abortion, when I was homeless?

I let off at the mouth, something I had never done in my life, "What did I tell you Bradley? Your holy ass mother would rather her husbandless daughter and grandchild live in a box, than to have it be seen by her fake ass friends. I know God is proud of the way you're handling this situation, cause that's exactly what Jesus would do, huh?"

"You know what, I changed my mind, you have two hours." Her disappointed glare changed into a blank stare.

I immediately called Leah to see if I could crash there for the night. She was so happy that I had gotten put out, she told me I could move in. She got her uncle's truck and was there to pick me up within thirty minutes.

****

Leah lived in a two-bedroom duplex. The first week was decent. We didn't see much of each other. She took classes at the community college and worked at the bookstore on campus. I was either at work or asleep.

"Do you have to work tonight?" Leah asked me.

"No, but I don't really feel like going anywhere."

"I don't either, but you been staying here for a week now and I feel like we haven't seen each other. So, I have planned a fun evening for us. We're gonna eat wings, do makeovers, take the quizzes in all of my Cosmopolitan Magazines and drink Grey Goose buddies!"

She had me at wings, I missed mommy's home cooked food though. The fun planned night, was a much-needed escape from my mind. Her makeover was more diligent and took longer than mine of course. Knowing nothing about primer, contouring and concealing, she literally put black eyeliner and red lipstick on me. She didn't know any better because that all that she wore.

A few hours into her drunken "niggas aint shit" rant she asked, "How come you aint touched that watery ass drink?"

"I'm pregnant."

"You're what?"

"You can have it if you want?"

"I don't want nobody's freaking kid! Are you crazy?"

"Not the baby, the drink. You can have the drink."

"How come you haven't told me? Does Twin know? What are you gonna do?" That was beginning to become the most annoying question ever. What am I gonna do? I didn't fucking know.

"No. I don't talk to Twin and I hate when you bring his name up. I hated that you even kept bringing me mail from him. Like, come-on we're talking about a guy who used to beat my ass daily. You could have sent the letters back to the jail or told the mailman wrong address or something."

"How are you turning this on me and you're the one hiding your pregnancy from me?"

"It just hasn't set in. It's hard for me to claim it. I guess I'm not ready to face it. But since I am an adult I think it would be ridiculous to feel like I needed to hide anything. I just found out the day you picked me up and I haven't seen you all week, so I'm telling you now."

"Well if you want to get an abortion, I could loan…"

"I don't want a loan, I'll be fine."

"How you bout ta be fine and you homeless? You bringing a kid into the world and not only is he locked up but he beats the hell out of you? I wish you would have told me that shit before you moved in here, because I don't like kids. Once again you back to not going out or having fun. How this nigga got a hold on you and he not even around?"

I flew to the bathroom. It was the first time I experienced morning sickness. She was right about a few things, but wrong about one. She said I didn't want to go out and have fun. Who said that was fun in the first place? Going out was her type of fun. My type of fun was setting goals and hitting them.

Things only got worse. Leah would sometimes get dressed in the living room and leave her clothes laying around on the floor. Dishes were piled up to the ceiling and the trash was never taken out. The bathroom counter was covered in weave and I just kept her bedroom door closed it was so disgusting. The funny thing was, it was spotless when I moved in. I wasn't sure if she was trying to make me uncomfortable or if she thought I was her live-in maid.

I finally gave in and cleaned the house top to bottom. Dusting, sweeping, mopping, and doing laundry, I put her apartment back together piece by piece.

"You seen my pink towel?" She quizzed, poking her head out of the bathroom door sending steam throughout the hallway.

"It's on your bed along with all of the clothes that were in the living room. I wasn't sure what you wanted me to wash so I did the towels and washcloths." I knew she would appreciate it.

"Yeah, so I'm a need you not to touch my things, please?"

"Well this place was disgusting I thought..."

"You thought wrong, you need to be thinking about your situation. I guess I need to put labels on things I don't want you to touch, including food." She slammed the door.

I knew I had to get the hell out of there, I just had to change my plan up. It would take a few more weeks. I gave up the day she invited over some mutual friends of ours. They all sat around throwing indirect comments that were meant for me. I heard Joy say, I don't see how bitches just lay up and get beaten on every day. They all snickered. One of them looked my way as if she was ashamed of the comment and I winked at her. I caught the drift. It was okay though; I knew God had something in store for me. The first step was getting up out of there.

Chapter 7

"Been Down So Long, It Look Like up, To me"

The next morning, I took everything I could carry along with me in a cab to the homeless shelter. A few pluses about the shelter was that I didn't have to be reminded about Twin, nobody thought they were better than me, and I had three meals a day. Depending on who donated that week, we would sometimes even have a snack, usually apples or peanut butter crackers. I still went to work every day with my head held high and not a soul knew that I was homeless. Doors were locked at 8pm, unless we had proof that we had to work. Having a curfew could be viewed as a downside but since I had nowhere to go besides work, I was fine with it.

My roommate was a lady named Tina. She was such an angel. She'd often stop me from cleaning our room, because I was pregnant. She warned me not to share or borrow any linen from anyone because bed bugs were at an all-time high. I didn't know they were a real thing, but I listened to her.

She would feed me words of wisdom, to bring me through my struggle. It was then, that I had a revelation of what my desires would be.

Tina would wake up before me. She worked in the soup kitchen mopping the floors and running the dishwasher. She would go down to the kitchen and have coffee with the staff members. Returning to our room around 9am, she would grab my hand in kneeling with her to pray. On our second day of praying she asked me to take the lead. I had never prayed out loud before. My mother was a prayer warrior and she took pride in it. I had moments where I would say, Lord help me find my keys or pray that our school might win a game. I didn't know what it meant to pray for something other than, things or position until I was homeless. More than anything I just wanted to have a spiritual connection with God, like Tina, and that was my new desire.

"What do I say?" I asked her. I was afraid I would lose track of what I was thinking about. The few times I had tried to pray, my mind would wander, and I felt no connection.

"You need to thank him. Look at it like this, what if someone called you, only when they needed something? How would you feel?"

"I would stop answering." I responded blankly.

"Exactly, but at the same Matthew 7:7 says **Ask and it will be given to you**. God wants you to ask him. He doesn't want you to ask him for gas money or food. You belong to him, why wouldn't he see to it that these things be done, if you are being faithful? Don't ask him for small things, that's insulting his mighty strength. Luke 12:24 says **Consider the ravens: they neither sow nor reap, they have neither storehouse nor barn, and yet God feeds them.** You must trust that you are being taken care of. God wants to do glorious, magnificent works in your life but he wants you to dare him. Have faith and dare him. But before you just go to asking him for anything, let's make a mental list of all that you are happy for and I want you to read the list every day before prayer. This brings humility and patience."

"Ok, well I'm happy I am alive. I'm happy my baby is still alive and that it is almost time to meet him." I couldn't think of anything else, what was I supposed to do, be thankful that I was in a homeless shelter. I laughed at the thought of it. "That's pretty much it."

"That's pretty much it? Are you serious?" Ms. Tina asked me. "Come up." She motioned for me to get off my knees, she leaned into me helping my, whale-of-a-frame, onto my bed. She pulled a wooden chair in front of me and sat down.

Tina gazed at me as tears welled up from her lids. I could feel my nose burning, I knew my tears would follow as well. Normally, I wouldn't have cried, because I didn't quite understand her reasoning. But, I was such an emotional wreck during my pregnancy, that I would cry at the mere sight of tears. Her grey twist hung just above of her chin. She had small black moles that scattered around her high cheek bones, decorating her eyes.

"What brought you here?" Ms. Tina asked me.

Wiping a tear from my left eye I answered, "My friend wanted me out because I am pregnant."

"So why didn't you go home to your family?" She studied my face.

"They won't take me."

"But, why Blake. You're smart and you are a great girl. Why do you think, that your family won't accept you?"

"My mom put me out when she found out that I was pregnant, out of wedlock. I went to stay with my friend, Leah, and once she found out I was pregnant she started," I caught my breath in effort to slow up the tear roll, *"making it known that I wasn't welcomed and needed to find a place to stay."*

"How so?"

"Like, I left work early one day because I had gotten sick. The only thing I wanted to do was go to sleep. About an hour into my nap, Leah came home and started slamming every door, drawer and cabinet. She ran water, turned all the lights on and played music loudly. I was hurting so bad that I didn't feel like getting up, so I called her phone. I told her I had to leave work early because I was sick and asked if she could keep it down a little? That was fair to ask, right?"

"Due your circumstances, of course." Ms. Tina adjusted herself in the chair, as she listened.

"So she says, I need to be getting all the hours I can get whether I feel good or not. That's the shit I gotta deal with while be pregnant, but I don't pay enough bills to just be laying around and leaving work."

"Every day it got worse and I became the laughing stock of all our friends. I began to forget who I was. I lost track of goals and began focusing on how to make it through the day. I even believed that I wasn't shit, excuse my language, but I still do."

I felt hopeless, the more I thought about the possibly of birthing a child, while living in the homeless shelter.

"So why would you come here? You had a roof over your head, I mean she wasn't the best roommate but she didn't force you to leave. You could have dealt with a sneak diss every now and then if you had a roof over your head, couldn't you?

Ms. Tina had lost her damn mind. My eyebrows wrinkled as I couldn't understand her point. "Uh, no. I mean, I would have stayed there if the streets were my only choice but, a shelter is better than that hell hole."

"But you still haven't told me why, dear."

"Why? I broke down in front of you telling you why. I'm in a place of vulnerability and you still don't understand? I wanted peace. I have had more peace here, in this shelter, in the same building as the guys who go out on corners begging for change. I share the same great room, with females who have bad hygiene because they found a pair of cute jean in the dumpster!" I stood up to make myself clear "about 75% of the population in this building is dressed in rags. I eat from the same pot as these people and guess what, I am at peace. I don't want it to end. I go to work happy, I'm finally gaining the weight I needed, for the health of my son, I'm focused and I will walk out a better woman than I walked in." I boomed.

"That's all I wanted to hear, sister. It's peace. God has a way of throwing you in the pit, to awake the spiritual you, so that you can die to flesh. Peace has always been there, you just had to ignite it. Now that you know that peace is more valuable than any**thing**, you want peace to be still. That, is how you pray. Tell him how thankful you are for everything that you have. Thank him for shedding his grace and having mercy on you. Ask that peace be still. Pray for everything in Jesus name." She offered.

I swallowed. I could feel another being, lift out of me. I could feel my underarms, and since I had gotten heavier, my crotch, perspiring. It felt as if the sweat that my glands were releasing, were parts of the old me, old thoughts and old ways.

As we kneeled by down to pray, my tongue couldn't be stopped. I lashed out against every demon and chain in my way. I thanked the heavens for my revelation. I was happy that I had went through what I had and that I had met Ms. Tina. I felt born again and was excited about my new journey.

Few weeks later as I got ready to move into my first apartment, I asked Ms. Tina if she would come stay with me. I had a three-bedroom apartment and wouldn't take no, for an answer. I figured, I would be the perfect hosts, since I had once been on the other side of things and knew how I didn't like being treated.

"Oh, no sweetie. You go on ahead and get what's in store for you. Our destiny is not the same. I can't go where you are going because, I didn't come from where you did. You're not the first who have asked me and you won't be the last." She smiled.

I asked her why she was so wise, yet homeless? She said that she believed that God, planted her there with purpose. She said she had helped many souls, in that very room and feared that if she left she would miss one. She said she had everything she needed there and no family left. I stayed at the shelter for five weeks and 3 days, before moving into my first apartment.

Chapter 8
On a Roll

Bradley paralleled parked in front of a small diner at about 8:50am. The Florida sun was easy on us that morning. We noticed the place was still closed. The ten foot windows worked their way around the corner of the sidewalk. *The Sound of Chow* was scribbled across a beige sign that hung over the building. The sun assisted in the peeling sign.

Chairs were turned upside down on tables, but I noticed a black guy sitting at a booth alone. I tapped on the glass door. Standing up with a handful of receipts, he towered over to the door.

"We open at ten." Holding both of his palms up to the glass door, to symbol the number ten, he flashed a golden smile. I eyed the man standing before us, he wore a grey t-shirt, black jeans and about three chains. He had four big cornrows to the back, that could use a touch up, none the less he was attractive.

"We're not here to eat, we are here to speak with Ashlee."

Displaying *the people's eyebrow,* he asked, "Who sent you?"

"A man named Kendrick, he's a realtor. He told me to come at exactly 9am." None of his damn business I thought. I just needed to see Ashlee. I didn't know her relevance, but I wasn't there for no reason, somebody knew something.

"Ole Kendrick, huh?" I noticed his eyes undressing us. "I'm gonna have to send my homie something for sending me a set of angels this morning?" I wasn't with the flattery; I was just trying to get to this chick. He was slowing down the process.

"Have a seat." he motioned to the booth. I slid in on the inside, Bradley sat beside me. He sat across from us, ignoring his vibrating phone.

"So what can I do for you beautiful ladies, can I get you some coffee?"

"No thank you, how long before she will be here?" I asked.

"Who?"

"Ashlee."

"Oh, my bad I'm so rude. I'm Ashlee and this is my restaurant."

"Oh," I blushed," I'm sorry."

"It's okay I've been used to this name for twenty-eight years. So, what's up?"

"Well, I was at a house party, well more like a mansion party in Miami five years ago."

"The Virgo Bash, that's my birthday party." He acknowledged.

Lord I was getting closer, "I got pregnant that night and I am in search of my son's father. I am not sure how you could be of assistance, but I went back to the home that you had the party at, and that is how I met Kendrick. Before you even ask, I do not know his name."

"Okay, no judgment passed, it happens." He laughed. "Do you remember what he looked like enough to describe even the smallest detail?"

"I'll never forget."

"So then, I'm safe, right? It wasn't me?"

"Absolutely not!"

"Whew, I did not need them problems right now. My baby momma bothers me enough. So, if you don't mind me asking, where was the deed done at? Do you remember any specific neighborhoods or maybe a car?"

"In the garage, of the house, that you had the party in. We were inside of a black truck."

His forehead wrinkled. I got nervous.

"Aw fuck! The other two cars were..."

"Gold, both were trucks as well." I finished his sentence.

"Wow. Those are all my trucks. My team drives them. My team consist of two people and one is female. Look out the window, you're parked behind the black truck right now. I can't believe this shit." He seemed pressed, as if he was the guy I was looking for.

"That only leaves one person. My right-hand man. Now that I think about it, I remember this shit. He spoke of you, well of...are you still dating that guy?"

"How did you know I was dating anyone?"

"He said, he figured that," he cleared his throat, "he could tell."

I dropped my head, "No, I am not, I've been single since that night." I dated two guys since, but we weren't exclusive, that was not his business. I could have sworn I heard Ashlee, mumble, bitch-ass-nigga under his breath, but I played it off, I was done with that conversation. I knew he was referring to the bruises on my back that night. It just reminded me of the note that I found in my mailbox.

"He spoke of you though, just in case you ever wondered." I smiled at the thought of him, but only the thought. The idea of him could be fun, but I'm afraid of glitter, because most of the time it's not gold.

"I know you got a picture of the boy?" Bradley showed him pictures of Zayden. His eyes kind of watered but a quick wiggle of the nose kept his masculinity. "He is definitely, my niggas son!"

"This subject might be too sensitive, for me to be the one who calls to let him know what's up. Respectfully, I can't give you his number or address. I can tell you that he no longer lives in Florida and that I'm going to visit him soon. I just feel better having you talk to his mom first. I'll let Ms. Peach take it from there. I will call her and explain everything to her, before you go see her. Ms. Peach is old school and might not feel the story coming from you, but she raised me. I know how to say it better." I gave him my number and hoped that she would call.

"So, what about shorty over here, I sure wish I had somebody to eat dinner with tonight. You ever ate at, *The Bus?*"

Bradley shook her head no. I walked outside, uncomfortable with seeing my little sister getting hollered at, so I gave them some space. I had other things to worry about anyway.

Chapter 9

Can't Get No Peace of Mind

Zayden, lie at the head of my bed, stuffed in my comforter, surrounded by a swarm of pillows. He threw back one piece of popcorn after the next. I lay sideways across the foot of my bed, propped up by my arm. Zay, thought I was on my laptop, but I was admiring him. He was so deep into *Toy Story*; he didn't notice me. I feared for his safety, knowing Twin was somewhere lurking.

I wondered how he got my address in the first place. In attempt to deviate my thoughts from Twin and focus on my business, I began checking my emails. I saw no mail for *Blake.Chanel*, just a few Old Navy promotions and one from D. Spencer, aka Twin. My heart plummeted. My fingers moved quicker than my mind in opening the mail. Don't look, don't look, I told myself. Too late, I had already finished reading what was typed.

Blake

I know that the paternity test was fake. I want to apologize for putting my hands on you in the past. You didn't deserve that. I know that you are afraid of me and you want to protect our son. No need to protect him from me, I would never hurt him. In fact, he is the reason that I want to do better. I don't know who you hired that would set up these fake ass test results, but it's only fair that since I'm out of jail, we take a real test. Besides, I know you never messed with anyone but me, so you need to stop fronting. I would love to try again with you and work on being a family for the sake of our son. I don't want him to grow up a screw up, because he has no father figure. If you don't want to work on us, that's fine too, but I deserve a legit test. If you don't honor me one, I can do it myself.

Twin was trying me, but I was no longer afraid of him. Time had healed my thinking and he had lost control of my mind. The only thing that I was afraid of, was my son's safety. I wasn't sure how far Twin would go at this point. I do know that if he believed that Zayden was his son, that he would not give up until he had proof. Even though he was issued a DNA test through the county jail, he thought the results had been rigged. I don't know what kind of connections he thought I had, but if I had that type of clout, he wouldn't even be alive. I knew that I had to get Zayden, out of Lehigh Acres. I also knew I needed a gun because I couldn't find a scripture for this one.

Chapter 10

As the Tables Turn

I drove to Fort Myers, while Zayden, stayed with Bradley. I knew I could call on Joshua, for a gun. I turned left onto Clearwater Ave, as I drove past a short thin girl who began flagging me down.

"Blake!" She just about broke her neck trying to get my attention. I slowed down and checked my rear-view mirror, trying to see if I recognized her. I didn't know anybody in Fort Myers, except Joshua, so I was shocked to hear her yelling my name. She jogged toward my car and I almost double over in laughter at the sight of this chick.

"Blake what you doin around these parts?" She asked. The past five years hadn't done her any justice. Her hair was in two unkempt braids to the back. She had on a pair of blue jeans and a long sleeved, white, t-shirt.

"Hey girl, I almost didn't recognize you!" I low-key dissed. Last I remembered of Leah, she wouldn't dare leave the house looking so dry. No makeup, not even an earring. She didn't look like she had been on drugs or anything, she just looked like she had, a dose of life.

"You feel like giving me a ride to the store?" I had some time to kill, and I didn't mind stunting on her broke down looking ass.

"Hop in." I moved my Nine West bag to the back seat as she slid in. I noticed she had on a new pair of Jordan's, so it wasn't that she did not have money, I just couldn't put my finger on exactly what it was.

"Girl, why you aint got no air on, it's hot as hell out here?"

"That breeze is feeling right, you are tripping. Why you got on them hot ass clothes is the question?" I quizzed, she laughed.

"I know, right? You look good as hell and this whip is the shit! I gotta get on my shit! Is that all your hair, or is it a wig? B, your shit was not that long back in the day!" she inspected. I was beaming with my, eat-your-heart-out facial expression, lips pursed, chin up.

"Girl thank you. I stopped getting perms when I was pregnant and I just transitioned to natural. I go to the Dominicans, for blow outs."

"That's what's up. You can park right here. I just need to run in and grab some cereal. Yall hiring at MAC? I hate paralegal work, they too damn nosy for me."

"I don't work for MAC anymore. I'm a business owner of *Blake.Chanel Cosmetics*."

"Fa real? Please hire me! I can't stand them folks I work with."

"My positions have been filled." I said proudly. My phone began ringing as she hopped out of the car. I put the car in park and answered.

"Hey Joshua, I'm right up the block, I gave a friend a ride to the store. Give me about ten minutes."

"You just gotta call me by my government, huh? I told you, it's Josh, mane. Plus, you don't know nobody round here. Don't be givin ees' hood rats no rides." He always spoke in a slur; I wasn't sure if he was high or if that was his natural voice.

"Be there in a sec." I laughed at him, unknowingly calling Leah, a hood rat, that she was. At least she had a diploma, that much couldn't be taken away from her, but she was definitely, a rat.

Hearing a vibration, I started looking around the seats, figuring Zayden, might have left his tablet in the car. I noticed a light coming from the passenger side door. I leaned over and saw Leah's phone. By the time I grabbed it, a notification preview of a text message popped up on her home screen.

DADDY: HURRY YO DUMB ASS UP FOR I BEAT THE...

I couldn't see the rest of the message, but I had seen enough to know that she wasn't wearing winter clothes to protect her skin from the sun. Wow, when the tables turn, I thought. I put her phone face down in her seat as she got back in the car.

"So where you on your way to?" She asked, while sitting four bags of groceries in the floorboard in front of her. She turned around and sat the milk on the floor board behind me. I watched her every move because my purse was back there and I don't play those types of games.

"I have a client that needed a home visit." I lied. She ran her mouth too much, to know that I was there to buy a gun to protect myself from, Twin. I was dreading that she would bring his name up. I figured it would be less likely, because they were neighbors, when she lived with her mom in, Lehigh.

"Take me back to the street you picked me up from. I live in that tan shotgun house with the toys in the yard." She directed.

"Toys in the yard? Not Ms. Leah, she hates kids." I reminded her.

"Look I do want to say, I am sorry about all of that, you know, the way I acted. I have three kids and they are a joy to me. I wish I knew your son. Bradley told me you had a boy. He should be my godson, but I fucked that up, I regret it too."

I smiled as warm as I could. I could feel the fakeness, in the muscles of my face. She had played me to the point of me living in a homeless shelter, while I was six months pregnant. The only thing she had to offer was a dry ass, sorry. She had me fucked up if she thought after all my suffering, I was about to let her ride on my coattail. I had come too far and was satisfied with only, showing her, what I had accomplished, in spite.

"Hey Joshua. I'm outside."

Joshua came strolling out of the bottom floor apartment holding his jeans at the waist line, as if they were heavy on his feet. He got walked over to my driver side window, leaning in, he said, "Where a nigga kiss at?"

"Do you have the guns?" I grinned.

"Straight like dat? You just using me for my gangsta. But I dig it, long as you know where to come." He slurred, with his sexy ass. I wasn't into d-boys but he could have had my nose wide open, if it wasn't for my son.

"First, I'm not using you, I asked to buy, a few guns from you."

"What if I said I aint want ya money?"

"Then, I guess I would have to go to the pawn shop tomorrow. They don't turn down money." Honestly I didn't have time to be waiting on a background check for a license, I needed protection right away.

"Damn B, I'm just fucking wicha."

Joshua was one of the two guys, that I dated after, I had Zayden. He was my first and last d-boy. He approached me in the produce section at, *The Market Zone*.

"Whachu you bout to do with those?" He asked me, pointing to the Ugly Fruit I was holding. He looked at me like I had two heads.

"Eat them." I tried keep from laughing. He looked so confused about my choice of groceries.

"Chu mean? You gotta steam it or something?"

"No, it's fruit, aren't you an employee here?" I wondered if his ignorance was real or if he was flirting.

"This my first day. I usually don't do the job thing, ya-ear-me." The way he said the words, "do you hear me" as if it was one word, made me blush. He was heavy set with a bearded face and pearly white teeth. Which was rare because, Fort Knox, don't have shit on a street dudes grill, in Florida.

"A nigga make his money in the streets, ya-ear-me? Why-onchu ask a nigga out or sum? You know he cute as hell?" He stood there with a khaki apron tied loosely around his waist, a pair of khaki pants and a pair of all black, Chuck Taylor's. Clasping his hands together like birdman he added, "Damn you gonna make a nigga ask you?" I busted out laughing. I could admit that I usually have a dry sense of humor so, to be able to make me laugh was a plus.

"Where are you trying to take me to?" I flirted with the idea of it, to see what he had in mind.

"We can go to a park or sum. Maybe, have a little picnic date, so you can show me how to eat this shit here." He pointed to my basket. I could have pissed myself I was so tickled. So, I gave him my number.

We had lunch the very next day. I wanted to take him shrimping so, I planned a lunch by the water.

"Man I don't like how them lil mufuckas be looking at me." He said as he dropped the shrimp in the bucket, off his line.

"Joshua, you have to pop the heads off."

"Man why? Why da hell am I popping da heads off these lil shits and I aint even bout to be da one eating em wichu?" He wanted to hint at the fact that I was going home alone. I sure wasn't going over his house, it was too soon.

"You might not be eating them with me, but you will be eating some at your house and you don't know the first thing about cleaning them." I explained.

"Shid, can't be nun mo than a rinsin. I can pay a dope fiend to bust the heads off, cause I aint with this shit, baby." He was such a teddy bear; I was so tempted to invite him over.

"Okay, that's gross as hell. I wouldn't trust a dope fiend around my food. FYI it's easier to clean, when the head busting is already done. Then, all that has to be done is cleaning the crap out of their backs."

"What you mean crap, like the nasty sea water and shit?"

"No, I mean like, shit!"

He gave me the same look as the day he was asking about the Ugly Fruit. I had developed a great habit of laughing around him. I pulled my shrimp off my line. I popped the head off and before throwing it in the bucket, I pointed to the shrimp, "See that long black string going through its back, that is shit. I slice it right there, and rinse that, out of there."

"Oh shit." He covered his mouth and widened his eyes. Man, I been eating that, my whole life, mane. Dis some bull shit fa real." I leaned against the rocky hillside holding on to the belly of my blue jean jumper as I doubled over in laughter. I laughed until my face was covered in tears. Not once did he crack a smile which made it even funnier.

We tried to have a date at least twice a week. When we weren't together we stayed on the phone all night. He asked me a lot of questions about Zayden and his dad. I told him I wasn't fond on Zayden's dad, to keep him from asking questions. I didn't like when he asked me questions about Zay, because I didn't want him to ask to meet him.

Two months had passed. The last time I saw him was when he said he didn't believe that I could eat more than him. He challenged that I couldn't eat one thing from each place in the food court at the mall, in one day. I agreed and met him at the mall.

Seated in a booth, I was working on my baked potato from, Wendy's. I had already made it through four places without, throwing up. I continued stuffing my face.

"So, when I'm a meet Lil Zayden. I know we been kicking it for a few months and you aint invited me ova or nun. I know, I'm, meet-the-kid material.

"Few means three, you mean a couple months." I corrected. "We just having fun, it's not that serious." I couldn't believe I said that aloud.

"Fuck you mean it aint that serious yet? You said you wasn't fucking nobody?"

"I'm not. But that's not because of you. I wasn't fucking before, I met you." I laid my fork down and began to stare at him in disbelief.

"So, what you saying is, I aint good enough to meet da kid?"

"I didn't say that."

"Well I'm offended." He won the bet. I had lost my appetite. We both said goodbye's and never spoke again.

Maybe I was too over protective of my son. I liked Joshua, he was charming in his own way. He was a little rough around the edges, he couldn't order from a menu to save his life. He was a loud talker and would sometimes joke on people to their faces with no regards. It was a treat for me to let my hair down and say what I wanted, without feeling judged. I was entertained and he wasn't a bad looking guy. All his kinks, could have been worked out. The problem I had was the fact that he only worked at the market for, four days. After that, he quit and went back to the streets. He said he felt that he stuck out like a sore thumb, they overworked him and he made more than his manager, by working on the block. I was bothered by his street life. He had to notice the way I would never get in the car with him. I wasn't trying to be at the right place at the wrong time fooling with him. I damn sure didn't want that for my son. I also didn't need my son getting attached to someone who, wasn't a sure thing. It was nothing against him but more of me protecting my son.

Bradley told me that my standards were too high and that's why I was alone. To me, loneliness was better than settling, just to be able to say that I had someone.

Present

"So, you been aiight?" Joshua questioned.

"I've been better. Clearly if everything was fine, I wouldn't be in a rush for a gun."

"Chick beef?"

"Nah, crazy-ex beef!" I kept it short.

"Aw man, that nigga on some fuck shit?"

"He's trying me."

"Mane, I know we aint a couple or nun, but I don't respect no nigga putting they hands on a b...female, ya-ear-me? I gochu. Just call me." He nodded his head toward the door of the apartment that he walked out of, as to signal someone. The door opened and out walked a white dude, carrying a Spiderman book bag.

"That book bag is for Zayden, I know you said he liked Spiderman. I bought it just for him, see the tags still on it. Them tools in there too, aint no bodies on em and you can have both of em. I can't make you pay for protection, from that week ass nigga." He said.

I pursed my lips together, feeling a whirlwind of emotions. Every time I thought about Joshua, I saw nothing more than a friend.

However, seeing him, always brought the weirdest feelings out of me. He remembered that my son liked Spiderman and that spoke volumes.

"I'm a just stick it in the backseat." I popped the unlock button as he slid the bookbag into the back-floor board. "That milk gone spoil before you make it home, unless yo AC be shootin out snowballs." He chuckled.

"Oh shit! That's Leah's milk. Let me go I need to run this to her."

"Aiight ma, do you mind if I call and check up on you?"

"My number never changed and I never told you to stop calling me." I winked at him while backing out of the parking spot.

****

I knocked on the screen door about ten times. A little girl with clear beads switched over to the door.

"Hi, is Leah here?" I asked her.

Putting her hand on her hip she sassed, "My mama said she aint here for none of the businesses ladies and yall can't take us away from her, cuz she aint even here right now." I saw about three silver caps shine through her mouth, before she pursed her lips together.

"Wow, and how old are you, little lady?" I checked for her age with her little grown butt.

"I'm finst ta be five in some months." She pursed her lips again. If she wasn't another Leah in the making, I don't know who she was.

I laughed. "Well, I am not the business lady and I don't want to take you. I gave your mother a ride to the store and she left her milk in my car."

Removing her hand from her hip, she folded her arms. "Ma-ma!" She yelled, looking behind her, "Mama, this lady say you left yo milk in ha car! She not no business...

"Fuck she mean you left some shit in somebody car, I thought you said you fucking walked?" Twin's voice boomed up the hallway. The hairs on the back of my neck stood as tall as the sun. Through the screen door I could see the hall but I couldn't see a person. I wanted to run but my fucking feet wouldn't move. I could hear banging and booming toward the back of the house. The little girls face saddened. I can take the milk, I have to go to my room and lock the door with my baby sister." She said reaching her hand out for the gallon. She shut the door and I left. The whole ride home, I couldn't stop thinking about that little girl.

I couldn't say that I felt for Leah, sure I had been through it and I wouldn't wish it on my worst enemy. It's just a lot easier to say what you would have done when you're on the outside looking in. Not empathizing with someone going through something like this is one thing, but to make fun of the victim and mimic them, is another. I might be a little fucked up to feel that she deserved what she was getting.

The thing that I couldn't get past, was that poor little girl. Not only had she been coached on how to answer the door ,but there was even a drill for her, on what moves to make, when Twin started hitting her mother. That had to be the saddest part for me. I couldn't imagine having that situation around Zayden, I barely even want to cry around him. I was glad to know where Twin resided. In the back of my mind I wondered if Leah wanted me out because I was pregnant or if she wanted her chance at him?

As I pulled into my driveway, I noticed I had a missed call and a text message from Ms. Peach, texting her address and telling me to stop by anytime but requesting to bring the boy.

Chapter 11

Sometimes You Just Know

"Whooaaa, I like when we drive down the hills Auntie Bradley."

"You do? Well, Auntie is gonna circle around and do it again how does that sound?" I shot her a look from hell, we needed to make it to Ms. Peach's house. She said she wouldn't be there long so we needed to get there. Two days had passed since we had met Ashlee and things were looking good.

"Son, I think it's time that you met your father." Bradley side-eyed me. We had already decided not to tell Zayden anything until we were sure that we could locate his dad and if he was willing to be in his life. I didn't think it was fair to blind side him though. It was a mistake that I had made and I would just have to take full responsibility, if things didn't work out. I felt it was only fair to at least, re-word the events that were about to take place. This way he wouldn't be blinded but wouldn't have his hopes up either.

"Really? Oh, cool!"

"Yes, but right now we are on our way to meet somebody very special, who may be able to help us find out where he lives."

"Awesome! Now I can learn the basketball, Auntie Bradley."

Even with Bradley looking straight ahead while driving I could see her grinning. She looked at me and smiled. "It's basketball Zay. Learn how to play basketball." She corrected.

The sting, I freaking hate the sting. It happened causing me to clench my nose to keep the tears from developing, I glanced out of my window to keep them from seeing me cry. I knew that my son was missing the key ingredient of becoming a man, his father. I wanted Zayden, to be able to live life to the fullest.

I wouldn't be like my mother, in keeping up appearances. Bradley told me that she wanted to get into the world of beauty and fashion. I told her to go for it. Mommy suggested that she do something more credible like becoming a doctor. Mommy already had a chance at life, but I found her trying to have a 2nd and 3rd chance at it, through her children. That isn't how I want to parent. I will not parent through society's eyes. I won't have them tell my son how he can or can't dress, how to speak, where to hang out who to date, that he must get married or what kind of education to get. I see Bradley struggling in school because she is not happy. I wouldn't dare put the stress of college on his back for him to study, graduate, find a job in an area that he didn't study in, and become overworked, underpaid and unappreciated. I want my son to find his passion and we will build around that. I sincerely hoped that his father turned out to be a great guy because I couldn't do it alone.

"Yes sweetie. Just sit your little handsome self here and enjoy TV. Here is the remote, I'm going to be in the other room with your mom okay?" Ms. Peach said to Zayden.

I kissed his forehead as Bradley and I followed her back into the front room. I introduced her to him as Ms. Peach, but after holding his face for a few seconds she told him, "I'm going to let you call me a name that no kid in the whole world has ever called me and its only for you because you have such a familiar face. Call me Gigi." My heart sang as I beamed of joy. She had accepted my son.

I stood, until she asked me to have a seat.

"Please." She insisted, motioning to an oversized French-styled Loveseat. The cream coloring on the pillows had me conscience about resting my back against them. The seat cushions were burgundy like the carpeting. The coffee table was oversized as well. Everything in the living room including the draperies was full of gold detail. A small pair of nursing shoes and a tan pair of moccasins, appearing to be similar in size, were lined up beside the front door. Next to the shoes, sat was a cream-colored sculpture of two elephants, one stood about 4ft tall and the other was about 2ft. The room wasn't well lit and kept me from studying her face. The smell of cinnamon grew stronger, but I couldn't find its source. Goosebumps treaded my arms as the AC overpowered the heat. About two minutes had passed and she still hadn't spoken. I knew she thought I should speak first but I wasn't sure what all Ashlee had told her. The awkwardness grew thicker as she cleared her throat. I turned my attention into the opposite direction, in search of confirmation.

"The one you're looking at, that's not his father, it's the other one." She said to me after I had focused in on a couple of photos of two young boys.

"How do you know which one I described to Ashlee if I've never said his name? What was he about seven or eight in this picture? He looks identical to my son." I objected.

"Because I know!" She snapped. Her voice never rose; her tone was only quickened. Again, she cleared her throat and tried to be easier, "because I know it's not him. He just happens to really favor his uncle that's all." She instantly claimed. Realizing that this had to be a bit much for her, I remained calm. I was comforted by how sure she was that my son shared the same blood as her. We were mute again as D.W and Arthur's voices echoed throughout the home.

"Well, do you have any recent pictures of him?" I asked for reassurance. I couldn't tell my son about something that I wasn't sure of, but I could tell him that I wasn't sure of something and those were two different things.

"I would if I knew how to use this stupid phone."

"It's actually a smart phone." Bradley interjected. It took everything in me to keep a straight face.

"Well, I guess we should go down and surprise him. He'll be absolutely ecstatic!" She clasped her hands together as she imagined our arrival. He's always wanted a son. He's single and he makes great money. It's been about two years since I've seen him so I would say this is a cause for a road trip." She crossed her legs. I despised her white pants. I thought they were jeans but they were cotton and her box shaped butt made them look horrible. "Do you need to discuss this with your significant other or anything?"

"Oh, no ma'am. I'm not dating."

"Well, I hope you don't think this trip is about rekindling a romance, because it's all about my grandson."

"Sure thing, Ms. Peach. Me being single is nothing new, I live for that boy.

"My son, has a lot going on, he barely has time for me, so…"

"I apologize for the way the order of events took place, but I can assure you that, I don't want your son at all. I was young when that whole situation took place…"

"Well, aren't you still young? Unless you're fifty, you are still young. Know, that you will continue to make mistakes, because you are a human being."

"You're absolutely right. My son and my business mean way more to me than my relationship status."

"Your business? Let me guess?"

"No need, I am a traveling professional skincare expert and professional MUA. I also have my own skincare line…"

"*Blake Chanel*?" we said in unison.

"You, are *Blake Chanel* from MAC? My daughter in law is *Blake Chanel*? Wait until I tell my bible study sisters. We went to MAC in search of you. An Asian lady told us that you had started your own line and told me to google you? I was trying to wait until pay day, because I would like your regimen also." Maybe, I didn't give myself enough credit after all. Sam did have my back. My brand would speak for itself and just maybe, God was fulfilling the desires of my heart, because I was doing, what he needed me to do.

Chapter 12

Excess Baggage

The moment we arrived in Nashville, my nerves were telling me that something was wrong. It just so happened, that the wedding party that booked me was only an hour away from where I needed to meet Ms. Peach and her son. I was just as nervous about meeting my son's father, as I was about my first gig. My business depended on my personality, my appearance, and the quality of my services. It needed to be as close to perfection as I could attempt.

The client had chosen the *Diamond Bridal Package*. This meant that not only would I do the makeup of the bride, but also her mother, the maid of honor and the bridesmaids. Also, they got the *Blake Chanel* steam-facials, for the bachelorette party. Being that the bachelorette and the wedding had a one-day gap in between them, I charged a three-hundred dollar *stay fee*. The gap day, that I didn't have to work, would be used to drive to Kentucky, for my son to meet his father. I hoped that he would be a standup guy, because I needed to get to the west coast and get my life settled, for Zayden.

Zayden and Bradley seemed to be enjoying themselves. I was glad because I was in my thoughts. We took a shuttle to the hotel where our rental cars would be delivered to us. Bradley planned on taking Zayden out, to explore Nashville. I was only there to close my past and explore my future.

After a long nap, I showered and dressed. I slid my *Blake.Chanel* smock over my head and grew proud. My nerves had settled and I was proud of myself. There I was, stepping out on faith with the sky to reach for.

Pulling my hair into a neat bun, I decided to go for a fresh face with only an SPF moisturizer. I was going to be doing facials and thought it was important that clients saw my clear skin.

******

As I was wheeling my cosmetics across the lobby floor the bellman asked if he could be of assistance and called me, Ms. Blake. I thought it was nice that the bellman went out of their way to learn the guest's names. I made a mental note to leave a great review and commend the gentleman.

After putting my luggage in the trunk, I slid into the driver seat and noticed a piece of paper on my windshield. I wasn't sure why

Bradley had written me a note, I got her text when I woke up saying that they were leaving. I grabbed the note and it read:

I'm here for my son

Love always

Twin.

"Bradley!" I screamed through the phone, "Where are you and Zay?"

"Over Mikelle's house."

"Who in the hell Mikelle?

"She was in class with me last year and transferred to, TSU to be here with her mom."

"Who else knows we're here?" I drilled her.

"Nobody, I didn't even tell mommy because she hates on you so bad. Girl what the hell is going on, you got me over here scared?"

"Bradley, Twin knows were here." I decided to whisper. I wasn't sure if he was in the vicinity. I was parked between two regular sized cars. I didn't see anyone around me.

"Do not go back to the hotel at all, I will figure something out and call you back, after this gig. Leave your ringer on. Keep an eye on my son, keep him close at all times, don't let him go into a bathroom without you and don't let him sit in the car with your friend, if you are not present."

"Oh my God, I know how he knows, I am so, so, so, sorry."

"What did you do?"

"I called Saint, to get Mikelle's number, I told him we were coming down here for a job that you had and I bet he told Twin. I thought Twin was locked up, Blake I'm so sorry."

"Who is Saint?"

"You know Saint, Twin's little cousin? You know him as Sinyarvis." We called him Saint in school. He used to date Mikelle."

I had to work. I couldn't be worried with something that was out of my hands. Furthermore, I wasn't about to let Twin block my blessings, the way he had in the past.

"Damn it! Okay, if Saint happens to call, talk to him the way you normally would and some kind of way, mention that our flight leaves at 2am to go back home."

Chapter 13

Passion Over Fear

Glad that I arrived before the drinking started, I set up my facial layout in the bathroom. I would work as fast as I could because I didn't have time to be dealing with drunk people, who couldn't hold their heads still.

All the bridesmaids at the bachelor party sat around in a circle playing, *hot seat*. The suite was dark and the ladies had only a flashlight. The person who held the flashlight had to answer a personal question. If they chose not to answer the question, they had to drink a shot of *Patron*.

The whole time I was working, I was at peace. There is something about pursuing a passion, that will make you forget about all the mess in your life. I was sad when I got to the last girl, knowing that it was back to reality, once I finished her. As a gift, each girl received my *Blake.Chanel All Day Moisturizer*, except for the bride. I bestowed her the entire skincare collection.

The bride to be was beautiful. Her dark skin was so rich, I complimented her and warned her never to use any type of chemical on her skin. I warned her to start using an SPF moisturizer, she giggled and said she was too dark to be worried about sunscreen. I chuckled at the thought process of us black women. I educated her on the dark spots and blemishes that come from the sun. I told her that neither sun burn nor skin cancer racially profiles us and will attack any color of skin.

****

Bradley met me at the car rental lot, so that we could change cars. I had her call Mikelle and ask her to grab our things out of our rooms. Bradley explained to her, that she was helping me and wouldn't get there in time enough to prevent being charged for another night. We told her if she could meet us at the car rental lot, we would pay her one hundred dollars and she agreed.

I then placed a call to the front desk of the hotel to tell them that Mikelle, would need a key made and to cancel the rest of our stay. I asked to speak with the tall bellman.

"This is Peyton; how can I help you?"

"Hi, this is Ms. Blake. Do you remember me?"

"I sure do!"

"Quick question, do you guys always remember the guest's names?"

"Oh, no ma'am. Sides the reglars, yers is the only one I knowed."

"Sir, how did you know my name?"

"Your husband, ma'am."

"I'm single."

"Mighty odd. This young fella said that his wife was here on a business trip and wanted us to make sure that your stay was as sclusive as possible." His slow talking ass irritated the life out of me, "He said that you liked to be knowed by the staff and whichever bellman called you by name we'd get fifty dollars at midnight. He asked me not to tell ya though. Sho'll hope you can keep it secret, I really need that tip ma'am." He whispered into the phone.

"So, you never considered any of that a little weird. Especially since you assisted us out of a shuttle, without him?"

"Well. Honestly, it didn't swang across my mind."

"Really? So, the thought of you possibly putting someone's life in danger, by confirming their presence never crossed your mind? This whole conversation has been recorded sir. If for any reason that guy rubs shoulders with me, I will report you to the police and have you fired. Anyone who needs fifty dollars that bad, needs their job. So here is what you're going to do, tell him that I checked out around 6pm and you personally helped me load into the shuttle. Tell him, I tipped you twenty bucks and that my job had been canceled and I didn't seem too happy about it. Tell him that the cars were picked up at about 7pm."

Chapter 14

Calling Audibles

I was beyond pissed off, hopefully my plan would keep Twin, at bay until my mission was complete. We ended up driving to a small city in Tennessee called, Clarksville. Per my GPS it was right on the borderline of Kentucky. This worked out just fine, because I was at a decent distance from where I needed to meet Ms. Peach and equally close to the wedding venue.

The city seemed more like a town and was a bit rural compared to Nashville. The hotel was only a three-star, but I was perfectly fine with it, as long as we were safe. I asked Bradley not to go exploring the city. She had been warned to stay off social media until we made it home. I knew she would be bored, but she knew that it was because of her, that Twin was on to us in the first place. To keep me at peace, she agreed.

I put on an ankle length, cream colored sundress, with a pair of brown gladiator sandals. I combed my hair down and trimmed my bangs. I decided again on a bare face and lip gloss. I wanted to be careful of Ms. Peach's eye, but also look the way I did upon conceiving, Zayden. I wasn't looking for a relationship per say, but if that same fire was there, I couldn't say that I would put it out either.

Honestly, nobody wants to be lonely. But who wants to be in an unhappy relationship? I dated someone for a little while after I stopped seeing Joshua. His name was Kelvin and he was dope as hell, at first. He worked at our local newspaper as an editor. He was fly all the time. In fact, I don't remember ever seeing the man in a sneaker. He never forgot to compliment me and was a complete romantic. He was affectionate, but didn't pressure me into having sex. He didn't give me the man-whore vibe either. I was feeling him until one night I made him a steak at his house and cooked it well. You would have thought I threatened his life, the way he reacted. Throwing the whole plate, upside the wall, he calmly asked me, if I had ever seen him order a well-done steak? I left and never looked back. I could deal with a lot of things, but anger and arrogance were deal breakers. Twin had left a great scar on me, mentally.

My GPS said that Zayden and I would arrive at the O' Charley's in Hopkinsville, Kentucky in twenty-four minutes. I figured this would be the best time to talk to him about it. Ms. Peach was supposed to arrive at the restaurant twenty minutes earlier than us, so that she could prep her son about, Zayden.

"Love, you haven't asked about your father lately. Would you still like to know who he is?"

"That would be awesome!" his little square face lit up. Rather than taking a chance on him not being at lunch, I just told him it would be after we ate. "Oh cool! This is the best day ever. It's even better than the rollercoasters." Hearing him compare his dad to a roller coaster was bringing that damn burn to my nose. I had to hold this pretty face together and be strong for my boy. No time for tears.

Chapter 15

Is You is, or is You Aint

"Seats for how many?" The hostess asked me.

"Um, may I borrow a napkin and a pen, before I decide, please? Ears." I stated pointing to my oblivious son.

She smiled handing me a napkin and a pen off the podium.

I wrote:

Me: *Supposed to be meeting and man and woman here, both black. I don't want my son to be disappointed if they didn't show up.*

Her: *there are only 4 tables occupied in the building. Only one table has a black couple, but they are sitting at a 2 seater and not expecting anyone to my knowledge.*

"Seating for two please." We followed behind the hostess. I noticed we were going to the same section as the black couple. I thought the hotel that I was staying at had done a better job at pretending they had no ill feelings toward black people. I scooped my sundress up and slid into my booth.

Zayden dropped his Spiderman and took off toward the lady sitting at the table next to us announcing, "Gigi, Gigi!"

I looked over to the lady and I'll be damned, if it wasn't Ms. Peach and her son, who, was not the father of my son, or was he? I didn't remember him having hair or being as chiseled. I studied his features as he studied my son. I looked over at Ms. Peach's lying ass. She hadn't warned him about a damn thing. He had the most puzzled look on his face and she looked like she could have been bought for a penny. I knew something wasn't right. The tension had wrapped itself around my neck like a boa and choked me with vulnerability. I became afraid for my son and his feelings. She continued hugging him, but wouldn't make eye contact with me or her son.

"Whose kid? He asked confused. "He called you Gigi, like grandmuva. You don't know anybody down hea in Kentucky." He frowned.

This man was unspeakable. His accent was beefy. He had neat, long dread-locks and I could tell by his lack of jewelry and strong demeanor, that he was indeed playing with a decent amount of money. He was doing it to me again. He could of have me right there in the booth if he wanted. I also noticed that he looked exactly like my son. He looked up at me and I couldn't get the image of us, *in the truck,* out of my head, but it only became clearer as he stood. I don't know why, but I stood as well. His eyes softened for me. I pleaded in apologies with without speaking. Even five years later, this was communication for us. The electric currents were so strong, that I was afraid of what would happen, if he stood closer to me. I could see his heart beating through his fitted black t-shirt. My heart danced as well. He missed me and was happy that I was okay. I could also pick up on the fact that my son hadn't come at the best time in his life. Stay strong for Zayden I told myself looking down at the floor.

"Yep, that is exactly what Gigi means. Did you know that Zayden? I am your grandmother and that is your dad. Kenyatta, officially meet your sons mother, Blake."

THE END

To find out more about Kenyatta, Read "The Lines of Loyalty" available on Amazon now.

Lines 2 Loyalty

Snippet: Kenyatta

"So, with that being said, I want to wish my round, my brother Kenyatta, a very happy life with his beautiful bride to be, Sevun. Aye sis take care of my brother don't let me hear you aint been keepin the homie belly fat and make sure he stays out of trouble. No disrespect to you Mike-Mike, but I'm the muscle behind this man and I can't help him all the way from Florida. These Kentucky cats don't play no games from what I hear." My dawg, Ashlee, flew in, to witness me get married to the love of my life. He was busy cracking jokes at the rehearsal dinner table, keeping the vibe straight. I was doing everything I could to appear unbothered. Sevun looked up at me a few times and winked. I struggled to wink back. In 24 hours, I could officially call, Seven Sabrina, my wife.

"Baby, eat your food. You know ya'll are about to be drinking and since you're not a drinker, you might want to put something on your stomach." Sevun said.

"I'm a grab a to go box and eat it the room tonight. You gonna be aiight, home alone tonight?" I spoke in a low tone across the table.

"Of course, I'll be fine."

"All alone, out in the country and you gonna be fine? Does fine mean, blowing up my phone?"

"Baby, I will be just fine. I was planning on going home and packing for the honeymoon, but I'm too tired. We don't leave for three days, so I'll pack later this week." I caught myself staring at ha. I don't want to ruin ha life. She deserves so much betta than this bullshit I'm about to bring to ha.

"What?" she blushed. After two years, I still could make my fiancé blush I'm gonna miss that.

"Nuffin. Ya skin is glowing ma." I whispered.

"Aw, thank you. We all got facials yesterday and I forgot to tell you that when Carmen left..." she rambled on and my mind left the convo. All I could see was images of ha leaving me. A part of me was like fuck it, don't tell ha. But, I knew I had to be a man and let ha know what was up.

"But, I'm wondering are you gonna be okay without me because by the way you're staring at me, I don't think you will last your first night without ya girl!" She teased. I grabbed her free hand from across the table. She pushed my dreads away from my plate, resting them behind my shoulders. I leaned in and kissed the top of ha nose.

"Look at the lovebirds down there." Mr. D made fun of us. He is my fawva in law. He faked his death for bout eight years. The whole time, dis nigga been living in Cali, getting different procedures done. From the pictures that I seen of him back in the day, he look like a whole different nigga. He aint even got the same ears. Lucky for Ms. Charlotte, she could feel like she was fucking wit a new guy. That nigga is certified seven-thirty, but dats my guy tho. We call him Mr. D, to protect his identity. He sat on the opposite end of the table between

Ms. Charlotte and Carmen. It seemed like once I moved hea to Kentucky, I inherited a brand-new family and we all love and take care of each ova. I know that in the end, they gone ride wif Sevun before they ride wif me tho. They are family, but to an extent. Only person at this table that was sure to hold it down for me, was my nigga, Ashlee.

Everybody began talking amongst themselves while my mind drifted off to her, not my fiancé tho. *Stop fucking up.* I kept telling myself. The last thing I want to do is end up a scummy like my fawva. As long as I'm talking to Sevun, I could control my thoughts, maybe I wouldn't be ok tonight without ha.

"I know I'm late, forgive me!" Who the fuck invited my muva, I thought, as she entered the private dining room at Ms. Quammie's Soul food restaurant.

"You made it moms." Ashlee stood up to greet her as she made her way ova to the table. Ms. Charlotte and Mr. D stood up to greet her as well. Ashlee introduced them to each ova. Just when I thought shit couldn't get any worse, she invites haself to my rehearsal dinner. She walked ova and hugged me. I mean mugged Ashlee. He frowned like he was confused.

Moms walked around the table and took an empty seat next to Sevun. I tried to remain cool.

"Sevun dats moms, mama dats Sevun." I tried to loosen the tight look on my face but I was fuming.

"Yay, mama you made it!" Sevun cheered. "Yatta said you were sick and you weren't gonna be able to make it. I'm glad you did, it's nice to finally get to meet you!" Sevun started talking and I tuned her out. I looked down the table at Ashlee and nodded for him to come wif me.

"Excuse us." I spat.

"What the fuck going on nigga?" I screamed on Ashlee once we got in the men's restroom.

"What you mean? Ya moms said she had met with you for lunch earlier. Plus, she tried calling you but your phone was dead. She said she needed the address to where we are, how was I wrong?"

Nigga, you know how she used to act when we brought dames around back in the day?"

"So! Nigga, this bout to be your wife, that's not the same. She knew them hoes wasn't shit back in the day."

"That's gonna make shit worse, B!"

"Man, lower your voice dawg." Ashlee suggested.

Lowering my tone, I said, "When she finds out I'm getting married tomorrow, she is gonna try to do whatever she can to run Sevun off. I'm the only son she got dats alive. She bout to act like she losing me too."

"Damn, Duetch. Yo moms don't know you getting married? Sound like she already lost you to me."

"Man, I got a whole ova thing going on dats even worse, I'm bout to lose my fucking skull, yo."

"Chill nigga. We don't call you Duetch for nothing. Believe me, whatever ya moms didn't know, she knows now. If she's mean to Sevun then oh well that's life, she will take it like a G. It aint like the lady is her next-door neighbor. Come-on bruh, you got good shit happening. Ya breads up, you bout to marry a fucking Goddess tomorrow, and yall getting ready to hit up Paris. You bugging. Now, I'm bout to take off I'll meet you at the suit, Vixen Evian and Twerking Tessa coming thru tonight. You know they bout to let us buss!" Ashlee left me standing there, still feeling like shit. I splashed water on my face and braced myself.

Walking back into the private dining room, I noticed everyone had left except my muva. I stood beside my chair, wif my hands in my front pockets.

"Park it, Kenyatta Maurice." I sat on the edge of the chair. "You look at me." I looked at ha clenching my jaw.

"Let loose of them damn teeth boy." I could hear the fire she was breathing.

"I'm sorry." I admitted.

"That you are." Ha voice cracked and I turned away.

"I said, look at me!" I looked back at a face full of tears. "Where do you even get off? Huh? Not only have you been planning a wedding but you're doing it tomorrow? You," struggling to express ha feelings she pointed at me, "are giving a stranger, my last name?" She pointed at ha self.

"Ma you came all the way down here unannounced and brought a chick that told you she had a seed by me, you didn't know my situation."

"That boy needs you."

"That boy hasn't been proven to be mine! How is that my seed? I aint took no fuc...I aint took no test." I roared while hitting the table. Ms. Quammie walked past the door way and glanced. I gave ha a stone stare and she kept it moving.

"Kenyatta, that boy looks just like you and your brother. You know that he is yours too. I saw the way you looked at him and I saw the way you looked at Blake." I love my muva to da core. She always been there fa us. I watched ha make a meal out of scraps. Once time I was mad at ha when she made me go to school in ha silver bubble coat wif fur on the hood of it, when I was in fifth grade. Yellow was laughing at a nigga, calling me all type of bitches. I couldn't wait to smack the shit out of em. I also rememba coming home from school that day, to my muva on the couch sick. I was already mad that I had almost killed about ten people fa laughing at me, my anger went through the roof knowing I had to make ha soup, walk ha back and forth to da toilet and make dinner fa Yellow and me. I didn't realize until I had gotten olda that she got sick from walkin us to school wif no coat on. It had to be below 20 degrees outside that day. She neva shivered one time. It was my fault that we even missed da bus in the first place. I love my muva. The only thing I wanted was to marry a woman who could exude half of the strength that she did. I saw that in Sevun. She was a grinder at heart and would give her all as long as the people that she loved were happy.

"I forgive you if you 'll forgive me?" She wiped her eyes.

"Of course, I do but how do I get out of this shit?"

"There is no getting out of it. There is no rejecting your blood. Don't forget about the way your dad left us. You saw him leave me to take care of you guys, by myself. You know what I went through raising you two with no extended help? I didn't even have a neighbor to make sure yall got in the house after school. I had to trust that you did and worry myself sick at work. I would wonder if Ken ate and if the doors and windows were locked? I wondered if I gave you too much responsibility and less of a childhood? I'm sure your son will experience the same thing, if you don't step in. Also, if baby girl really loves you she will accept Zayden as well." I agreed with zero percent of what she was saying. I already knew that me popping up wif a kid would be a deal breaker fa Sevun. I knew that without a doubt...

Lines 2 Loyalty

Coming soon
to a kindle near you

Follow Brittany Pitteard's author page on amazon.com or goodreads.com Please leave a review and thank you!

Made in the USA
Middletown, DE
09 April 2017